secrets

EMMA BRAY

one

Zane

MY NAME IS ZANE CULVERT, and I have a secret. Well, two secrets, actually.

My first secret?

I know all of Anne Johnson's secrets.

I know that her mother sent her to kindergarten a year early just to get her out of her hair while she fucked the johns that paid her rent.

I know that because of that, Anne was always the youngest and smallest one in her class and that she always felt left behind and mostly stuck to herself throughout grade school.

I know that she threw herself into her studies, graduated early, and started attending college at seventeen instead of eighteen, hence why she's the youngest fully licensed elementary school teacher in the city.

I know that she's really the face behind Charlotte Locke, the famed naughty romance novelist.

I know that despite her erotic writings, Anne is really a virgin.

Thank God for that. Really, it saves me a lot of time and aggravation. I don't have a list of men to kill now. She really did the world a service by retaining her innocence.

I know that she still feels guilty about her mother's death. It wasn't her fault at all, but she feels like she should have done more, sat with her more in the hospital as the cancer at away at her body.

That's natural guilt, I suppose. When someone you love dies, you'll always feel like you didn't do enough, like there was more you could have done—no matter how much you did.

That's what I've heard anyway. I don't know from firsthand experience seeing as how I've never cared for anyone enough to care when they died.

One of my many character flaws, I suppose. A lack of empathy, the psychologists had called it.

Makes me perfect for working the unsavory jobs I do on the streets, dealing with the dregs of society.

But the nature of my work isn't my second secret.

No, my second secret?

My second secret is this: Anne Johnson is my obsession. I watch her every second of the motherfucking day.

I've been watching her for two years now. I suppose "stalking" is the technical term for what I'm doing, but I don't like to call it that.

Stalking sounds so...devious, calculated.

And while I am those things—and frequently—that's not the case when I watch Anne.

When I watch Anne, I *feel*.

I feel so many things. Despair, desire, lust, pain, anxiety, fear. I feel more than I've ever felt in my pitiful excuse for an existence.

She gives me a reason to exist. Watching her, protecting her, guarding her from afar. She is my purpose in this life.

Anne Johnson is my everything.

And she doesn't even know it.

I've thought of approaching her many times. God knows how much I long to take her in my arms, hold her against me, run my fingers through her auburn hair and along her milky white skin just to see if she's as soft as she looks.

I want to cherish her, see her smile, be the cause of her smile, feel her light shining down on me. Have her blue eyes peering up at me behind those tortoiseshell cat-eye glasses she wears.

I would die of happiness at just one look from her.

This feeling that grips my chest and tightens it every time I think of her—much less look at her...

I don't know what to call it. I've determined that it must be "love." Something I never thought myself capable of feeling. I'm still not entirely sure I'm capable of it.

And there are so many definitions of it, depending upon who you ask. All I know is that I feel like I'll die if I don't see her every day, that I'd give my life to protect her.

I'm perfectly content to sit and watch her sleeping for hours.

I've got cameras rigged up all throughout her apartment. I have a tracking device on her phone. I frequently sneak into her apartment and read her diary, catching up on all the thoughts in my beautiful little Annie's head.

That's what I call her secretly.

My little Annie.

There's nothing I'd rather read than her innermost thoughts. Some might call me breaking into her apartment, reading her diary, and keeping tabs on her everywhere she goes an invasion of privacy, but I can't help it. Everything about her fascinates me.

I feel closer to her than anyone else on this entire planet.

And she doesn't even know I exist.

I stroke my finger over her face on my phone screen where I have my live camera feed of her pulled up.

She's curled up on her side, her hands in little balls under her chin as she slumbers peacefully.

Like a pretty little kitten.

When did I "meet" her?

It was monumental and yet it wasn't. Nothing super big happened and yet it did. What I mean is there weren't any extraordinary circumstances that led to our encounter.

I was just jogging through the park one day, doing my regular routine.

It was starting to rain. People were hauling ass to get back to their apartments, but I was enjoying my run.

A little rain never hurt me. In fact, I like it when it rains because then the park clears completely out. I get a sick sense of satisfaction at watching all the park-goers scurry away like mice seeking shelter.

I rounded the bend in the track, and there she was.

She was several feet up ahead just sitting on a park bench serenely.

Completely unbothered by the fact that she was getting drenched.

Her eyes were closed, her face slightly tilted up as if she welcomed the droplets on her face, the wet waves of hair plastered against her cheeks, neck, shoulders, and arms. The little gold dress she had on was plastered against her skin, wet against her creamy thighs that were glistening with water.

She looked peaceful and yet sad all at the same time. Something about the vision she presented wrapped its fingers around my neck, cutting off all my air. I couldn't breathe there for a moment.

And for the first time in my life, I couldn't move.

I stopped dead in my tracks and just stared at her.

I'd never seen anything more beautiful. And I'm not just talking about her physical beauty.

No, it was more than that.

It was her soul, her aura, her essence, whatever the fuck you want to call it.

It was breathtakingly, heart-stoppingly beautiful.

I don't know how long she just sat there in her own little world, her eyes closed. I don't know how long I stood there staring at her, but I eventually got my wits about me enough to move off to a line of trees where I could continue to watch her undetected.

From that moment on, I followed her. I found out everything I could about her. I've shamelessly manipulated circumstances so that I can keep an eye on her at all times.

And the more I found out about her, the tighter my chest got, the deeper my obsession grew, until I'm drowning it.

But I don't want to be saved. I want to drown in her.

I keep telling myself that this is enough. Watching her is enough.

I know I could easily slip into her apartment while she's there, satiate my longing to feel her skin and run a hand along her hair and cheek while she sleeps.

But I don't. I know that one taste of her will undo me.

If I touch her one time, I don't think I'll ever be able to let her go.

And I'm not worthy of her. I'm darkness, and she's the purest light. My hands are dirty, and I don't want to taint her with all that I am.

But, fuck, how I long for her.

I pull my dick out of my joggers and begin stroking it quickly while I stare down at the screen. I hold the hair scrunch I grabbed from her apartment up to my nose and inhale deeply.

Oh fuck.

Her sweet raspberry scent fills my nostrils just as I come, shooting sticky ropes up onto my stomach with a grunt.

All it takes is her scent to send me over the edge. If I ever had my cock actually inside her, I'd probably die.

Or at the very least embarrass myself by ejaculating immediately like an overeager teenage boy.

My phone buzzes, and I regretfully close out of the camera feed of my little Annie to check the incoming text.

Unsurprisingly, it's a client wanting another "favor."

I pocket my phone as I rise and get ready to go to work. Even though I know she'll be sleeping, I can't go more than a few hours without having to check the feed to check on her.

Until tomorrow, my sweet little Annie.

two

Anne

MY NAME IS ANNE JOHNSON, and I have a secret. Actually, I have a lot of secrets, the biggest being that I write dirty romance novels in my free time.

I write under a pen name, of course. We can't have the city finding out the person behind the steamy Charlotte Locke novels is actually an elementary school teacher.

That probably wouldn't go over well with the parents or the board.

Especially since my heroines are usually always virgins, and my heroes are alpha males who take what they want. *The Romance Digest* has rated my book's sex scenes with five peppers, the spiciest sizzle rating you can get.

Want to know what's ironic about that?

I've never had sex.

I'm still a virgin.

Yep. A twenty-two-year-old virgin.

I don't really have a clue what I'm talking about. Yes, I understand the mechanics of sex, and a well-described sex scene can get my panties wet and my pulse racing.

But I've never had an orgasm.

I don't truly know what I'm writing about when I write about that white-hot release. I'm only saying what the characters tell me to say.

Imagine the world's shock if everyone found out that I, a virgin who has no first-hand experience with sex whatsoever, is the one churning out such realistic sex scenes.

Imagine what the parents and board members would say if they knew that I'm the one writing what they would no doubt deem as filth.

But here's the thing. They're all hypocrites

because according to the astronomical sums I get from my royalties, someone is reading the hell out of my books.

They sell like hotcakes.

So much so that I don't really have to keep teaching, but I do it anyway. Why? I ask myself the same question all the time. To keep up appearances? Because I truly do love the kids?

Or, maybe it's because I know that if I wrote all the time, I would eventually truly, completely succumb to my fantasy worlds and just live there.

I'd go insane.

Writing has always been an outlet for me. I've been keeping diaries since I was a little girl, and I still keep one.

But it can also be dangerous for me. I'm too fantastical, as my mother used to put it. I get too wrapped up in my imagination and can't separate what's real from what's fantasy.

Teaching, having a "normal" job keeps me grounded.

But writing frees my soul.

I type out the final sentence of my latest manuscript and adjust my glasses as I peer at the screen critically.

La fin.

No sooner is it over than another plot is bubbling up inside my head.

I sigh. This is how it goes with me. No sooner do I get one idea out than another one is taking its place. Some might say it's a vicious, never-ending cycle.

I quickly jot down the basics of the next story, though I don't do a strict outline. I'm not a rigid plotter. I let the story unfold before me. I let the characters lead me. It's like embarking on a journey with new friends, and I'm often-times just as surprised as the readers to find out where the characters take me.

For me, writing is like interactively reading a book.

I spend the next hour jumping into chapter one, and by the time I finally still my typing fingers, I see that it's way later than a teacher should be up on a school night.

I sigh and close my laptop before I remove my glasses and run a hand through my hair.

My mind is still buzzing, the characters braying at me, wanting to get their stories out, but I try to calm the chaos within me with some deep breathing exercises that are supposed to quiet the mind.

I push my pajama bottoms off so I'm left only in my panties and a cami. Then, I crawl under the covers and let exhaustion overtake me.

three

Zane

I STIFFEN within my jeans when I see her the next morning. Christ, but she dresses more like a sexy secretary than an elementary school teacher. I never had such a hot little piece for a teacher in grade school, anyway.

My eyes sweep her from head to toe, taking in the navy pencil skirt and sky blue button-up she's wearing. The color of her top perfectly matches her eyes. It enhances them, making them appear even lighter behind those tortoiseshell frames that only bring out the hint of gold in her hair.

Next, I scan her shapely calves, my eyes falling down to rest on the sensible navy pumps she's wearing. They're classic and close-toed with a nice heel but nothing too outrageous. How I'd love to caress her calves, those legs thrown over my shoulder, those shoes on her feet as I drive deep within her, making her mine.

Mine. She should be *mine.*

That familiar ache of longing lodges deep in my chest, and I take in a shaky breath as I begin to follow along behind her—at a distance of course.

This is our weekday morning ritual. I meet her like this and walk her to school. She doesn't live far from the institution she works at, but there's no way in hell I'm taking any chances with her safety. I shadow her every step of the way to make sure no one messes with her.

I'd burn this whole city to the ground if someone hurt her. I'm not being dramatic either. I'm motherfucking serious. One hair on her head gets harmed, and I'll blow this whole place up.

So, really I'm doing a human service by following her and making sure she's okay.

Once she's safely inside the building, I retreat to a more secluded location in the park near the school. I lounge on my usual bench with my legs stretched out in front of me and pull up my feeds inside the school.

Yeah, I know it's illegal to bug a school, but ask me if I give a fuck.

I only bugged her classroom. I can tap into the cameras already in the hallways and common areas, but the school doesn't have any cameras in the teachers' individual class-rooms, and I can't very well leave Anne alone all that time.

I can't stop the smile that pulls at the corners of my lips as I watch her teaching her students. She smiles at them kindly, and there's a light in her eyes as she pays each student individual attention.

It's obvious from the adoring way they look up at her that they worship her. And I can't say I really blame them. I worship her too.

She takes them through math, English, and social studies, and then the bell rings for lunch.

I watch her walk over to her little personal fridge where she keeps some premade salads and fruit. It pleases me to no end that she mostly chooses to stay in her room and eat her lunch alone rather than join the other teachers in the teacher's lounge.

I grab an apple out of my own pocket and take a bite out of it, sharing this lunchtime with her.

My hand tightens on the fruit when a knock sounds on her door. I frown, pissed off that someone is interrupting our time together.

She walks over to the door to see who it is, and I drop my apple, my vision blurring red for a moment, when I see the pompous fucker on the other side of the door.

"Ron," she greets him in surprise.

"Hello, Anne," he purrs as he leans in her doorway.

My lip curls up into a sneer.

"Can I help you?" she asks in confusion. She makes no move to step back and allow him entry into her classroom, and I mentally cheer her. *Good girl.*

"Actually, you can," he practically croons down at her. It couldn't be more obvious what the fucker really wants. He was just hired last week, and I've had my eye on him. Something about the way he looked at my Annie the first time he saw her told me he was going to be a problem.

"I packed way too much lunch and wondered if you'd like to share it with me."

Anne looks surprised, but then she smiles at him. My anger flares up at her smiling at any man. I'm partially mollified when she shakes her head, though. "I'm sorry, Ron, but I've already got lunch." She motions over to her desk where her half-eaten salad sits.

I glance back at the fucker smugly. *There. Take that. She's clearly not interested.*

To my mortification, he pushes off her doorway and pushes his way into the room, brushing his body against hers before she has a chance to fully step back and give him entry.

"That's okay," he says, "Mind if I just keep you company then?"

She frowns for a moment, but then she schools her features and relents, "Okay."

She's too damn nice, my Annie. She doesn't do well with saying no to people, never wanting to hurt anyone's feelings.

I grit my teeth as the prick pulls a chair right up next to hers behind her desk.

I damn near cheer when I see her sit gracefully in her own chair and roll it a bit away from him, though. *Good girl.*

At first, she seems to just suffer through it—politely of course. She glances longingly at her computer screen, though. I know her fingers are itching to type out more of the story she's currently working on.

Something this guy would never understand about her. But I do. God, I do. I understand everything about her. And while I've never been a big romance novel reader, I read every one Anne publishes.

Because it's a part of *her*. *She* wrote it. It came straight from her imagination. Her innermost thoughts.

And Christ what an imagination she has. I'm unashamed to admit that I've stroked off many a night to the dirty scenarios she comes up with in her books, only in my mind the heroine is replaced with her and the hero with me.

Anne might not have any firsthand knowledge of sex, but I know what she wants, what she fantasizes about. It's all there in her books like a sexual map to her pleasure.

And God how I would love to give it all to her, take her to the heights of pleasure she fantasizes about.

At some point, the fucker begins wearing down on her. I clench my teeth. He's beginning to charm her. I notice her smiling more. My stomach drops as her smiles become more genuine and she laughs, a light tinkling of bells.

Hot jealousy spears my stomach. She *laughed* for him. I feel irrationally betrayed. She doesn't even know I exist, yet I feel the knife of betrayal sink deep into my gut that she laughed for another man.

He's grinning back at her stupidly, his chest puffed out like a proud peacock preening for a female.

Idiot.

My hands shake with murderous rage as I study him.

Sandy blond hair, brown eyes, muscular build. I suppose women might find him attractive. He's not as tall or muscular as I am. I can guarantee you that.

Anne laughs again, the sound bubbling up from her chest. His eyes drop down to her chest and darken with lust.

Mine darken with rage.

He lays his hand atop hers where it sits on her desk.

That's it. This fucker is dead.

As much as I feel the need to lash out at something, I fight the urge and force myself to watch the rest of their interaction until lunch is over and he leaves.

Good thing for him he doesn't touch her again.

When the students file back into her room, I finally close out of the feed and stand abruptly.

I make my way over to the gym where I train and head straight for the punching bags.

I've got to work some of this aggression out before I explode.

My jaw is clenched so tightly my teeth ache.

I hit the bag over and over again until I'm dripping with sweat.

I can't get the image of his hand on hers out of my head.

Every time I think of it, I pound the bag with renewed vigor.

Finally, I calm enough to think.

And I suddenly know what I have to do.

It's time for Anne to meet me.

four

Anne

I'M on my way home, furiously typing on my phone, jotting down ideas that have popped into my head throughout the day, when I suddenly smack into something solid.

"I'm sorry," an apology is already on my lips before I ever look up.

A deep chuckle and a, "No, I'm sorry," draws my eyes up over a broad, heavily muscled chest, a thick neck corded with muscle, a strong, lightly stubbled jawline, a smiling mouth surrounded by lush lips, and straight into stormy gray eyes that are crinkled around the edges with obvious humor.

I clutch my phone tighter in my first as I stumble, more from the shock of the gorgeous man before me than from the collision of our bodies.

Collision of our bodies. God, that's a good line. I have to remember to jot that down in my notes to use in a future book.

He reaches out a strong hand to steady me with a firm grip of my elbow.

I'm blushing like the inexperienced virgin I am at his touch. Sparks sizzle along my skin where his bare flesh meets mine, and I smile nervously up at him. "It was totally my fault. I shouldn't have been texting and walking."

"Not quite as deadly as texting and driving." He flashes me a full smile, and my breath catches at the beauty of it. The man is a Grecian god. Actually, that's not right. He's too dark for that. He's more like a sexy demon because he invokes thoughts of nothing but sin. Like seriously, with that dark lock of hair that wants to fall forward onto his forehead, those smoky gray eyes, and his ripped build, he could be the model on the cover of many of my romance novels.

I somehow manage to stop gawking at him long enough to clear my throat and say, "Still, I'm a sidewalk hazard."

He chuckles again, and my eyes don't know where to look—at the rise and fall of his chest, his crinkled eyes, or that sinful mouth.

"Really, though," he says, "I'm the one who ran into you. Why don't you let me make it up to you over a cup of coffee? I know this amazing little place over on fifth..." he trails off, raising an eyebrow questioningly.

My mouth falls open as I state the name of the place.

He looks taken aback. "You know it?"

I laugh. "Of course! It's my favorite coffee shop in the whole city!"

"What a coincidence," he smiles again.

"Indeed," I agree.

"Well, what do you say...?" he pauses again, obviously prompting me for both my name and answer.

I bite my lip as I consider. I see his eyes hone in on the movement, and it's probably just my imagination, but I think I see them darken for a moment.

I blink, and the look is gone, though.

I've obviously been writing too many romance novels.

I chew my lip for another few seconds. This is crazy, right? Having coffee with this guy I just met?

It's like...like...

Something out of one of your romance novels, a little voice whispers in my head.

"Come on," he coaxes teasingly, "I hear they've got the best toffee nut latte in town."

My mouth falls open again. "How did you know that's my favorite drink there?"

He just shrugs. "It's my favorite drink, and you look like you have good taste."

That elicits a laugh from me. My inner me is hissing, *If you don't go with him, we'll make your life a living hell from here on out. Come on, girl! He's perfect! Drop dead gorgeous, kind, funny, and he loves your favorite coffee shop too. You'd be an idiot not to jump at this chance.*

For once, I don't tamp down that inner voice with the sensible one that's been drilled into my head by society.

Instead, I place my hand in his outstretched one. "Anne. My name is Anne, and sure. I'd love to grab a cup of coffee with you."

His smile widens as his hand tightens around my own. Something like victory sparks in his eyes, but again, it's gone almost as soon as it appears, replaced with smiling warmth.

"Zane," he offers me his own name before he begins leading me down the sidewalk to our favorite coffee shop.

Maybe instead of writing everyone else's romance story, it's time to finally write my own.

five

Zane

A SMUG SMILES tugs at my lips as I watch my little Annie getting ready for bed. She's smiling, and it fills me with a sense of pride that I'm the one who put that smile on her face.

She has a dreamy look in her eyes, and I feel something I've never felt before take wing inside my chest.

Hope.

It's a light, floaty feeling that's completely foreign to me.

I don't quite know what to do with it.

I was the perfect gentleman with Anne. I held the door open for her, paid for her coffee, asked her about herself as if I didn't already know everything, walked her to her door. I was dying to kiss her, and there was a moment there when she turned those pretty blue eyes up at me that I thought she wanted the same.

But she just met me today, and I don't want to rush things. I don't want to spook her.

Plus, I'm honestly afraid once I get my lips on her, there will be no going back.

I don't know if I'll be able to stop myself from owning her completely.

I didn't do more than hold her hand or place my palm against the small of her tiny back, and even those meager touches were enough to have me stiff as a board in my pants.

I frown and feel that tightness return to my chest, though, when I think about Anne asking about me. Of course she'd been curious to know more about me. What I do for work. I told her I'm a consultant, which isn't a lie. I just didn't specify *what* kind of consultant. How old I am. Thirty-two. Ten years older than her. She didn't seem to mind, thank fuck.

I run my thumb along my bottom lip as I contemplate how our relationship is going to go. Relationships are built on trust and honesty—or so I've heard.

How am I ever going to tell her how long I've been watching her? My stomach sours just at the thought of her finding out about the cameras I have in her apartment. I know my Anne, and I know she's not going to be happy about that if she finds out.

So, what do I do? I finally have the girl of my dreams within my grasp. Do I keep my obsession from her forever? Won't she run as far away from me as she can get if she finds out how I've invaded her privacy?

A cold sweat starts to break out on my forehead just at the thought of it. I can't ever let her run away from me. I'd have to track her down and kidnap her. I can't live without her.

I can't.

I get anxiety if I go too long without checking the cameras to see her.

Once she's tucked safely into bed, I close the feed and head out to take care of a few jobs.

First, though, I have a little stop to make.

To a certain young teacher who had the audacity to touch what's *mine*.

six

Anne

I PRACTICALLY FLOAT into work the next day. My dreams were filled with silvery gray eyes and strong muscles. A deep voice and dark hair.

Zane.

I blush just thinking about him.

He seemed so perfect at the coffee shop. Everything I could have ever dreamed in a man. The way he focused his sole attention on me like I was the only thing on this earth that mattered, despite the cute little waitress who kept trying to get his attention in vain.

The way he stared directly into my eyes like he was looking straight into my soul. He seems to truly know me. Like no one has ever known me.

That's crazy, right? We literally just met. How can I feel so connected to someone so instantly?

And the way his gaze kept darting down to my lips throughout the evening...the way they would darken as they looked at me, taking my breath away...I just knew he was going to kiss me.

But he didn't.

I was simultaneously relieved and disappointed. I'd wanted his kiss, but everything already seemed so intense, I didn't know what I'd do with it if I got it.

And Zane is such...such..a man. He's in his thirties, so I know he's more experienced than me. I'm sure he's had plenty of skilled lovers. I can't bear the thought of him being disappointed in a virgin like me if we ever...if we ever...

My cheeks are flaming, and I press my

palms against them to try to cool them down before I walk into the school building.

I see Ron up ahead and start to give him a little wave and a smile. As much as I hadn't wanted a lunch guest yesterday, his company had actually been pleasant. He's witty and fun to be around, and I think he'd make a good friend even if I'm not interested in him romantically.

He's definitely no Zane.

However, as soon as Ron sees me, this curious expression passes over his face before he turns on his heel and starts heading the other way.

I frown, wondering if I somehow offended him yesterday. He seemed fine when he left my classroom at the end of our lunch break.

I mentally shrug and continue down the hallway. Oh well. I don't have the time or desire to mull over his strange behavior.

I lose myself in teaching my students, praising their progress and wondering at the magnificence of young minds. When children are as young as my kindergarten class, their minds are like little sponges. They suck up information so quickly. It's truly amazing.

Before I know it, the lunch bell is ringing.

For once, I'm not itching to write. Instead, my thoughts are on Zane and how we're supposed to meet for coffee again this afternoon. I get butterflies in my stomach just thinking about it.

I go to my refrigerator to pull out a salad, but before I ever reach the appliance, there's a knock on my door.

My heart trips in my chest when I open my door and find the object of my daydreams standing right in front of me.

"Zane!" I can't keep the surprise from my voice. "What are you doing here?"

He looks halfway sheepish when he says, "I know we were supposed to meet for coffee later, but I couldn't wait that long. I had to see you again. So, I brought the coffee shop to you."

He holds up a to-go cup of my favorite toffee nut latte.

A flush creeps up my neck at both his words and the intensity in his eyes.

I take the proffered cup and step back to let him into my classroom. "No, that's okay. I'm glad you came. I wanted to see you too."

His eyes seem to light with satisfaction at my admission.

We walk over to sit at my desk. I can't help but notice how his eyes don't waver from me the entire time. He doesn't glance curiously around the classroom.

His attention is fixed solely on me, like he's drinking in everything about me.

He was just as intense yesterday.

And I love that, but I don't know what to do with it.

My hands are trembling as I bring the coffee cup to my lips and take a sip. His eyes never leaving mine, he does the same.

A drop of coffee glistens on his bottom lip, and I don't know what comes over me, but before I even realize what I'm doing, I lean in and press my lips to his, swiping my tongue along that creamy drop, tasting both it and him.

He's perfectly still, so still that I'm afraid I've moved too fast and offended him. Oh god, what if I read everything wrong and he's not interested in me that way?

I start to pull back and apologize, but

before I can, he hauls me to his chest and crashes his lips down onto mine.

And good lord, the way he kisses me...

It's like he's dying and I'm the oxygen keeping him alive. He's sucking the air straight from my lungs, mating his hot tongue with mine.

Tingles snap along every nerve ending in my body, and I clench my legs together as I'm suddenly throbbing in that most private of places.

He definitely notices because I feel his hand moving under my skirt and cupping my mound through my panties.

"This is mine, isn't it, sweet girl?" he breathes against my lips before he starts licking and sucking at my neck.

I don't even stop to think of how odd his possessive words are after having known him only a day. All I can focus on are his hot lips and wet kisses on my skin, leaving fire in their wake.

His finger strokes along my slit through my embarrassingly wet panties. "So wet for me, aren't you, Anne?"

That finger slips beneath my panties and

begins to rub my clit. And oh my god, the pleasure has me whimpering and digging my nails in his shoulders through his shirt.

"Poor girl," he whispers, his voice husky with lust. "I bet you've never had a real orgasm before, have you?"

My cheeks color. How does he know? Yes, I've stroked myself before and tried to achieve that bliss, but I never could.

"I'm sorry," I find myself mumbling.

He gently lifts my chin with the hand that's not stroking my wet folds.

His eyes blaze into me as he croaks out. "Don't be. I love that you're innocent. I want to be all your firsts."

I want to ask him how he knew, if I just have "virgin" tattooed on my forehead or something, but before I can, he captures my lips in an achingly tender kiss as he finally breaches my hole, pushing one finger up into me while his thumb continues to work my nub.

"Oh my god," I moan into his mouth. I feel so full, and the pressure that's building within me is delicious, but it promises something even more amazing.

"Yes, baby. Let it happen. Let me take you there."

I listen to his voice crooning in my ear and clear my mind, just allowing the sensations to pass over me.

And then I explode, my innermost muscles convulsing and sucking on his finger greedily.

"Yes," he hisses in my ear as he continues to stroke me through my release. "So mother-fucking beautiful, sweetheart. You're so precious."

Only when I'm completely limp in his arms, slumped forward against his chest does he pull his finger out of me.

My cheeks heat when he brings his finger that's glistening with my juices up to his lips and licks it all off, his eyes never leaving mine.

"Best cream I've ever tasted," he comments with dark eyes before taking a sip of his coffee.

I can't help noticing the huge bulge in his pants, but the bell signaling the end of lunchtime chooses that moment to sound.

I bite my lip and look up at him. "I'm sorry," I apologize to him again. "I'll have students coming in soon."

He cups my cheeks and places another

tender kiss on my lips. "Don't worry. We'll finish this later," he promises.

I nod vaguely and watch as he stands and adjusts himself before exiting my room. I'm still in shock over the fact that I kissed him, and he gave me my first ever orgasm here in my classroom.

He turns when he gets to the doorway and gives me one last lingering look full of promise.

And I'm already counting down the minutes until the bell rings at the end of the school day.

seven

Zane

IT'S a heady sensation to have the object of your obsession finally in your arms. I don't know how I stopped myself from ravishing her right there in her classroom, but somehow I did.

I'm finding that I'm suddenly able to do a lot of things I didn't previously think myself capable of—and it's all because of her.

Like slitting that fucking prick teacher's throat. Somehow I knew Anne wouldn't be okay with that, so I let him off with a warning.

One that I'm pleased has scared him shitless. I told him when he saw Anne coming, he better walk the other way from now on, and I saw he obeyed this morning.

Anne doesn't need any other males in her life but me. I'm too territorial and possessive to share her—even with a male friend. Some might call my views insane and archaic, but I can't help it. They're lucky I don't throw her over my shoulder and haul her away with me caveman style. Lock her up and hoard her all to myself like the finest treasure.

I'm stretched tight as a rubber band as I wait outside the school for the bell to ring. My cock is heavy and aching, eager to pick up where we left off.

I have to wait for the trickle of students flooding through the doors to fall off before Anne finally comes through the door herself.

My heart stops when she steps out into the sunlight, the light glinting off her auburn hair, her glasses perched prettily on her pert little nose.

Her eyes meet mine, and I see the same hunger roaring through me reflected in them.

Fuck me, how did I ever get this lucky?

Her heels click across the sidewalk as she hurries over to me. I'm moving toward her too. We're pulled toward one another like opposite ends of a magnet. I don't think we could stop this if we tried.

And then she's throwing herself into my arms, and I'm catching her, instantly smashing my lips down onto hers to taste her.

Sugar. She tastes like pure fucking sugar. Every. Damn. Time.

She gathers her wits before I do, pulling back from me and causing me to growl a sound of protest.

"Not here," she whispers against my lips, her eyes darting around as if checking to see if our blatant display has been overseen by any parents or faculty. I don't really give a fuck if it has, but she's a teacher, and I know she has an image to uphold.

"My place or yours?" I ask her, my breathing ragged, the need raging in me so hard I can hardly see straight.

"Which is closer?" she asks me, her own voice sounding strained. Fuck, it doesn't help me knowing she's just as on edge as I am. It makes me want to mount her right here in the middle of the street, fuck whoever sees.

"Mine," I manage to rasp out before I grab her hand and begin leading her to my apartment that's only a couple of blocks down from hers. I purposefully got the place to be close to her so I could be there in no time if she needed me. As much as I wanted to get one in the same building as her, that would have been too great a temptation. I've kept her close but not close enough that she would happen to see me.

Neither of us speaks. We're both walking quickly, half panting in anticipation of what's going to happen once we get behind closed doors.

I'm too impatient to wait for the elevator. I stoop and lift her into my arms before hauling her up the stairs.

My hands are shaking by the time I get to my door and place the key in it to open it.

So close. So motherfucking close.

Anne's wispy little breaths are hot and heavy as I open the door, and then I yank her inside and cage her in against the wall, pressing my body flush against hers, needing the contact.

Fuck, she's all softness, and I can't get enough of her. I'm ravishing her mouth as I run my hands all over her, inching up her skirt. I don't even bother unbuttoning the buttons on her blouse. One yank has them popping free.

She gasps at my impatience, and while I'd planned on going slow with her, I can't.

Plus, I suddenly know that this is the way it's meant to be with us.

Hot and fast and furious. It's all she writes about. My girl might not even realize it herself, but she doesn't want it soft and romantic. She needs it hard and real and raw, and that's exactly how I'm going to give it to her.

She's tugging on my shirt, but I stay her hands. "I don't think you're ready to see that yet, honey," I tell her.

She gives me a curious look, but I distract her by taking a nipple into my mouth and sucking on it.

She moans, her head falling back against the wall, her legs falling open.

I press my hardness right against the apex of her thighs and begin to dry hump her while feasting on the little rosebuds that are her nipples.

"Zane," she chants my name over and over again, and I feel moisture leaking in a steady stream from the head of my cock.

"Christ, if I don't stop, you're going to have me nutting in my pants like a little schoolboy. See what you do to me, Annie?" I growl into her ear, half insane with lust.

"Don't stop!" she pleads.

But I do. I have to because nutting anywhere but inside her sweet pussy is unacceptable.

She lets out a whimper of protest, but when she hears me unzip my pants, she licks her lips and her lust-filled eyes find mine.

"That's right, baby. I'm going to give you exactly what you want. You ready for my cock, sweetheart?" My words are coming out half-slurred, and it's no wonder. I feel drunk, intoxicated by her.

"Yes, yes, Zane. I want it," she tells me unashamedly.

I rip her panties clean off her body and look down to see her thighs glistening. "Christ, you're soaked for me, baby."

She makes a keening sound, and I can't take it anymore. I have to be inside her. *Now*.

She's so wet the head of my cock slides in easily, and I almost pass out from how tight she is. I could bust right now before ever breaking her hymen. I grit my teeth and tense up every muscle in my body as I struggle for control.

But then Anne does something completely unexpected. She thrusts down with her hips and slams herself onto me, yelping out as she breaks her barrier, and then I'm encased completely in her hot, wet pulsing heat.

"Oh fuck, oh fuck, oh fuck, baby. That little snatch is gripping me so tight. Oh fuck, I can't hold on." I begin jabbing up into her furiously. I can't control myself. I can't stop this. Oh fuck, she feels so good.

Her pussy is milking and sucking me like nothing I've ever experienced before, and then she's screaming out as I feel her fall open all around me like the sweetest flower budding.

The fluttering of her pussy is too much for me to take. I feel my spend traveling up the stalk of my cock, and I already know it's going to be a massive load before I feel the rush of it pop through my tip.

I come violently like my soul is being ripped out of me. I jet pulse after pulse into her until I don't think my balls will ever empty. The force of my seed shooting inside her sends her spiraling into another orgasm. I stare down at her beautiful face, marveling at this amazing, horny, little virgin.

When I'm finally spent, she collapses against me. I stroke her hair back and place a protective kiss against her forehead, marveling at the fact that she came so hard she passed out.

With my cock still planted firmly inside her where it belongs, I carry her to my bed.

She's mine now.

I'm never letting her go.

eight

Anne

I WAKE up alone in an unfamiliar bed. The soreness between my legs sends the memories of what happened between Zane and me rushing back to me.

I don't remember coming to this bed, and I flush when I realize I must have passed out after my second orgasm.

I go over to Zane's closet and slip on one of his shirts, inhaling deeply, loving the way his scent envelopes me.

I hear the shower running and make my

way over to the bathroom, a smile curving my lips at the thought of joining him under the running water.

His shower door is clear, and he's standing under the spray with his back turned to me. I take a moment simply to admire his backside, the strong muscles in his back, his perfectly formed butt, his thighs like canons.

Zane is crafted from marble. Beautiful.

He turns and pauses in surprise when he sees me standing there.

My breath catches when I see the ink decorating his chest, but then they narrow and widen as I realize what the tattoo is.

My name. It's a huge tattoo of my name plastered right across his chest.

He turns the water off and wraps a towel around his waist without drying his hair or chest. He walks over to me slowly, his eyes pinned on me warily like I'm a skittish animal that might dart away from him at any moment.

When he's standing right in front of me, I reach out a shaky hand and trace the tattoo. It's not fresh. At all.

And we've only known each other two days.

Two days.

Which means...he had to have gotten this tattoo before we met.

Which means...what exactly? What does this mean?

His words from earlier come back to me. *I don't think you're ready to see that yet, honey.*

"Zane?" my voice is barely a whisper asking him for an explanation.

Something in his eyes has me backing away from him.

He looks pained at my retreat, but something inside me is telling me to run. At the same time, something else inside me is screaming at me to stay.

I'm so confused, but I obey the first instinct and turn on my heel, heading out of the bedroom and through the first door that I see.

And then I stop dead in my tracks.

Every book I've ever written is on display along with various photos of me. A monitor is showing the empty inside of my apartment.

Various items that I thought I'd lost are laid out on a table.

Oh my god.

Zane's been stalking me.

That's how he knew I was a virgin. That's how he seems to know me better than anyone else. He knows my deepest secrets—the things no one else knows.

He's been studying me.

My stomach churns as the questions burn through me.

"How long?" I ask. I don't even have to turn around to know he's right behind me.

He doesn't answer, so I ask my next question, the one that's really burning me. "Are you just some sort of twisted Charlotte Locke fan?" Tears prick my eyes at the thought. "Was any of it real?"

I thought our meeting was serendipity, fate, destiny. But it's all been a lie.

He orchestrated all of this. I feel played, deceived. What an unwitting little fool I've been.

He grabs my shoulders then, turning me to face him.

His eyes are blazing with remorse and denial as he vehemently denies the accusation. "No! It's all real, Anne. Us, we're real. Nothing else matters. Yes, I know your dirty little secret. I know you're the pristine teacher by day but the naughty writer by night. I know how your fingers itch and burn and you can't settle until you get the stories out. And I know why they do that too. Because you weren't getting what you needed. But, honey, I'm here to feed that little thing between your legs so you'll never have to feel that way again."

Despite his admission, something about the wrongness of his words makes my thighs clench up. God, I still want him. My body is still throbbing for him.

He sees it too because he kisses me desperately. "I stole trinkets from you to feel close to you. I snuck in and read your diary because I wanted to know everything I could about you. I watched you every second of the day because I felt like I'd die if I couldn't see you. I had to keep you safe."

He breathes all this against my lips before he finally pulls back and looks me straight in the eyes. "Yes, Anne, I know all your deepest secrets. So, let me tell you mine. I saw a girl sitting in the rain one day. She was so beautiful she took my breath away. I've watched her for two years, falling deeper in love with her every day. I never approached her because I knew I wasn't good enough for her. Until one day I couldn't take it anymore, and I had to try. I'm obsessed with her. And it's not because of her books or her looks or anything but her."

He grips the sides of my face. Tears are streaming down my cheeks, and he brushes them away.

"It's you, Anne. *You*," he rasps. "God, don't leave me, sweetheart. Not now that I've finally got you in my arms. I'll burn this city to the ground. I swear to God I will. I won't survive without you, honey."

He seems broken, his eyes wide at the thought of me leaving, and even though I know that according to society what he did was wrong, if I'm honest with myself, I'm flattered. Flattered that he's cared about me enough to silently watch over me all this time.

My heart breaks at the thought of him pining all this time and thinking he wasn't good enough.

And I'm grateful. Grateful that he finally did show himself to me.

It suddenly doesn't matter to me. I'm going

to embrace this man, this love, this connection between us. I felt it from the moment I met him. It's everything I've been writing about and more.

And I suddenly realize that I haven't had that constant compulsion to write since I've met him. He's right. It's because now that I've got him, he's calmed that storm inside me.

He knows me better than I know myself.

He took all my secrets, and he kept them and cherished them. He cherished me.

I stand on my tiptoes and press my lips to him, communicating to him in my kiss all that I feel for him.

He wraps his arms around me and pulls me tightly against him, deepening the kiss, kissing me with all the intensity of our secrets laid bare.

epilogue

One Year Later

Zane

I LAY my hand on my wife's pregnant stomach, loving the feeling of our child kicking in her belly. Anne traces her name on my chest, something she often does when she's deep in thought. I let her concentrate. While I know she doesn't have the same near-constant compulsion to write as she once did, she still enjoys writing, and I'm pretty sure she's planning out her next plot. She has that little furrow in her brow that means she's seeing events unfolding in her mind.

She writes full-time now, though still under her pen name since the mystery of it seems to be part of what has readers eating out of her hand. I still do consulting, but I've gone legitimate. No more unsavory jobs in the dead of night. I run a legitimate business that my wife and child can be proud of. I've done every-thing I can to be the man Anne deserves, though she knows all my darkest secrets just like I do hers and loves me anyway.

"Is there oral in your upcoming novel?" I ask her, my voice coming out husky and my cock already hardening at the thought of tasting my wife's cream.

Her blue eyes flick up to me, and she grins. "Yes, I'm pretty sure there will be."

"Have you written the scene yet?" I ask her suggestively.

She shakes her head slowly. I see her nipples pebbling through her thin white cami.

My own grin turns wolfish. "Why don't we write it together now, then?"

She bites her lip, already knowing what I want before I drop to my knees in front of her.

Her legs fall open easily, revealing her panty-less pussy under her skirt.

I inhale deeply, savoring her scent, before I fall on her mound, licking and sucking with a vengeance.

I feel her fingers nest in my hair as she gasps and begins to grind herself against my stiff tongue.

Her hormones have been crazy since she's been pregnant, and I love it. One swipe of my tongue has her turned into a horny mess, and I love nothing more than to feel her squirt her sweet juices all over my face.

My cock is so hard it's leaking, and I pump my hips, fucking the edge of the couch as my wife rides my face to her orgasm.

When she creams on my face, I shoot my load in my pants, unable to hold back.

We both moan in unison.

This is her new writing process now. I help her write her new scenes. When we first met, we acted out every scene from all her books so many times, it's no wonder she came up pregnant as soon as she did.

And I plan on putting many other children

inside her. I want to tie her to me as many ways as I can.

"Zane..."

"I know, baby." I stand and go get her laptop for her, knowing she needs to get her inspiration out.

She smiles at me gratefully. "You know me so well."

"Mmm-hmm," I agree. "All your secrets are mine."

She laughs as she adjusts those little cat-eye glasses that I love.

"And yours are mine."

Indeed they are. Always.

Our secrets are ours.

And to hell with what the world may think of any of them.

THE END

Connect with Emma!

Visit Emma's website to get a FREE book you can't get anywhere else: www.authoremmabray.com.

www.ingramcontent.com/pod-product-compliance
Lightning Source LLC
Chambersburg PA
CBHW031132160726
47989CB00017B/2903